First published 2017 by Two Hoots
an imprint of Pan Macmillan
20 New Wharf Road, London N1 9RR
Associated companies throughout the world
www.panmacmillan.com
ISBN 978-1-4472-7401-8

The right of Emily Gravett to be identified
as the author and illustrator of this
work has been asserted by her in
accordance with the Copyright,
Designs and Patents Act 1988.

135798642

www.twohootsbooks.com

For Sonny

A CIP catalogue record for this book is available from the British Library. Printed in China
The illustrations in this book were created using pencil and watercolour paint.

His Nana had knitted it for him when he was little.

It was warm and cosy, and it kept his ears toasty.

It was an . . .

OLD
HAT!

So Harbet got a new hat.

The latest hat!

It was fashionable, fresh and fun.

It was low in fat,
high in fibre, and
could provide 80%
of his daily vitamins.

It was the latest,
most up-to-datest
hat there was.

Until . . .

It wasn't.

HA HA

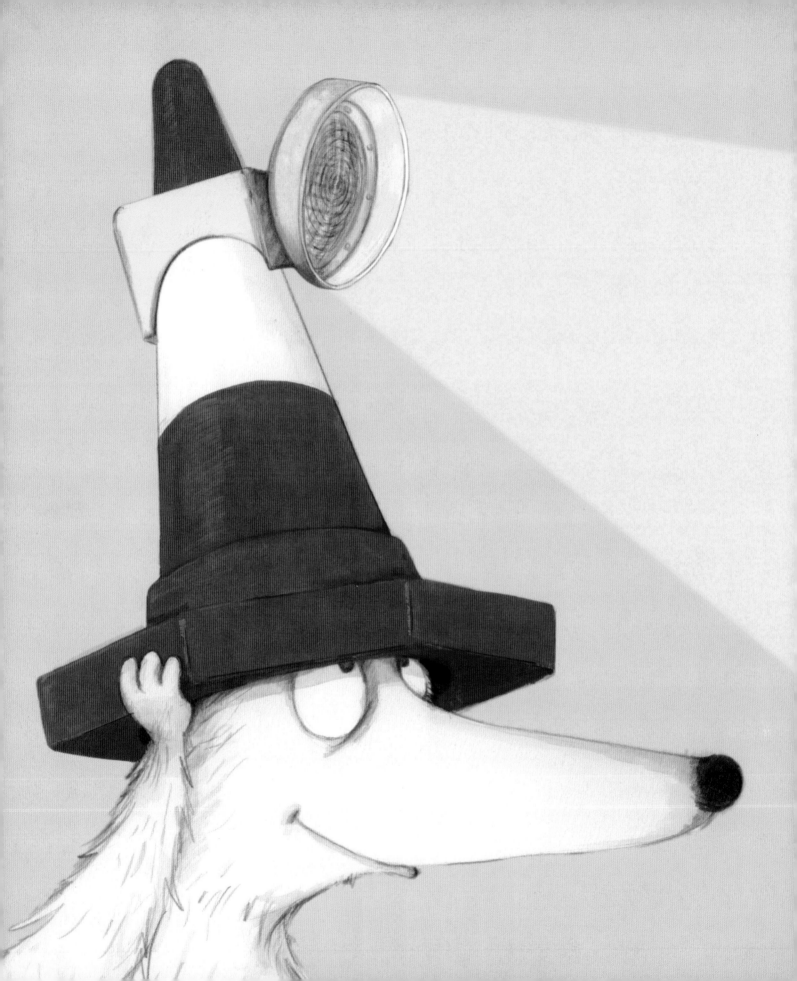

So Harbet got a *new* new hat.

This hat really was the latest thing.
It came with a state-of-the-art flashing light
and was highly visible to oncoming traffic.

But when Harbet put on his hat and went outside . . .

Harbet was determined to have the latest hat.
He bought 'Top Hat' magazine,

and was the first in line at the hat shop
on Hat Unveiling Day.

But whatever Harbet tried . . .

OLD HAT! OLD

HAT! OLD HAT!

Harbet had had enough.

So one day he did something no one had ever done before . . .

Harbet took off his hat.

My best Old Hat
SAVE FOR WINTER

FRAGILE